WARRIORS ON THEIR KNEES

ODY UDEM

Ody Ventures Nigeria

ISBN: 9798818709994

Cover design by: Ody Ventures Nigeria

All scriptures are from New King James Version

Published and Marketed by: ODY VENTURES NIGERIA 22 Osadebe Street Ogui New Layout Enugu Nigeria 08034617855, 08025942028

To our wonderful and caring Mothers: Vicky Oyiboka Okeke, Mary Udem, Joy Ojechi and Vicky Nonyelum Ifediora.

If we live in the Spirit, let us also walk in the Spirit.

BIBLE (THE KING JAMES VERSION) - GAL 5 VS 25

CONTENTS

INTRODUCTION

You do not fight for victory, you fight from victory, knowing fully well that the devil has been defeated. Beloved, do not pray with a mindset of attacking humans with your prayers, the devil is the enemy and not human beings. Attacking human beings with your prayers goes against love which is the basic principle of the New Testament Church. Again you do not pray as if the devil has not been defeated. (Words of Daddy Sam Osaghae)

It is discovered that if for example, you are praying against the idols of your father's house, the enemy can manipulate the other members of the family and so they tend to see you as their enemy. Beloved, you know what that means?

As a committed Christian on this planet earth, you are always fighting battles whether you are aware of it or not. You have to be among the warriors on their knees, for the Bible in 2 Corinthians 10:4 told us that the weapons of our warfare are not carnal, but mighty through God to the pulling down of strongholds.

You tend to see smoke on the horizon and then feel your heart pounding in your chest as you hear the war raging all around you, what do you do? You can feel the fear of failure but you choose to be courageous and so you raise your shield, lift your sword and fall to your knees to fight.

Why do you fall on your knees? Because when you fall on your knees you can now fight like a warrior, calling on the name of the One that is a Conqueror. For you are more than a Conqueror when you believe and fall on your knees.
Brethren, do you know that the enemy trembles every time you fall on your knees like a warrior? for he knows that the battle is no longer yours.
In my book Rachel Weeping, I was urging mothers to rise and cry for their families, but this time around, I am calling everybody to arise and chase the enemy away from the family. Enough is enough.
You are broken and weak, God can hear you. Though the enemy roars like a lion, the main Lion of the tribe of Judah is on your side. He will go before you and behind you, fighting on the left and the right.
Your weapons are trust and hope in Jesus your Defender, He is the King of kings and Lord of lords. He said, "I am with you, do not be afraid. I have already won the battle."
Beloved, always remember that when God's warriors are on their knees, the battle has just begun, it is not yet over until you meet your Father in Heaven. You just have to give God your weakness and He will give you His strength.
I have come to realize that stars cannot shine without darkness around, and as stars of God here on earth, we ought to fight amid the darkness.

The most significant words in the Bible are these by our Lord; "And you shall know the truth and the truth shall set you free." That means, if you do not know the truth, you are not free, you are in bondage.
The problem is that some people do not even believe that there is a problem. In some families where there are some mysterious activities of the devil, the people will not listen

to you because they are not seeing what you are seeing. Neither are they hearing what you are hearing. Many a time this leads to the untimely death of loved ones. But what will you do? When you are the only one crying "wolf" when they believe there is no wolf, it is very unfortunate and only the fervent prayer of the righteous will save the family.

For too long the Church has been told by her ministers that the devil does not have any power. But then we feel the pain of reality when a child is taken from us through death or a husband leaves for another woman. Then our eyes try to open a bit. The devil is highly organized and he has monumental plans of heartbreak and death for you and your family if you do not know how to stop him.

All the same, the Bible told us in Revelation 12:11 that we overcome by the Blood of the Lamb and the words of our testimony. When we remember the finished work of Jesus Christ on the Cross of Calvary, we stand to fight the enemy. Always remember that the Bible said that "no weapon formed against you shall prosper and every tongue that shall rise against you in judgment, you shall condemn." Prepare to wage war against the devil and his cohorts.

You will learn, if you have not already, that one of the primary reasons the devil sends tribulation and problems your way is to keep your mind away from God and the work of His Kingdom on earth. If you are overwhelmed with problems yourself, you will never feel like interceding for anybody in prayer. Not to talk of helping others with their problems.

Discipline yourself to pray no matter what happens each day. This is one of the greatest weapons you have against the Dark Kingdom. But you must learn how to pray effectively and in detail. Also, pick out several people who need help and begin to pray earnestly for their needs.

Become like Christ by giving the needs of others first. Wake up each day with the thought of doing some positive things for the Kingdom of God. This attitude will also help you to develop a positive perspective in life and get you out of the rut of just existing each day.

Discipline yourself in prayer and the study of the Word, look for a place and create opportunities to be a blessing to other people. As you do these things, you will find that God will meet your needs in your own life without you asking. This is a spiritual principle – when you take care of God's business, He takes care of your business.
Thank God for the precious gift of the Holy Spirit and prayer. The Holy Spirit is even sounding the trumpet for the battle, are you ready to answer the call?
Beloved, if you are not genuinely born again, please go to Repentance Page and pray the prayer there, before you continue. You cannot successfully fight the devil the way you are now, without casualty.
It pains me so much that when you tell some people what the Lord is saying about them, they tend to take God for granted. They feel they have arrived, so why listen to you. A brother was told to pray that someone sacrificed his money to the marine kingdom and he was nonchalant about it.
Listen and listen good, you may have two houses, one in the city and one at home, three cars, a booming business and what have you. But in God's record, you are supposed to have a house in the city, a beautiful one at home, three Estates where some widows and orphans have free accommodation, twenty cars to be given to people and five houses built for widows at the village. Can you now see the difference? That was why the Bible said that my people perish for lack of knowledge. You cannot claim to know

everything; it is not possible. The things of the spirit are reserved for those that are called and they answer.

Remember that nobody is qualified, the only thing is that God calls the unqualified and makes the person qualified to do His work.

I just want you to make up your mind now, this book is in your hand and you will always fight on your knees until you recover all you have lost. For emphasis, I will say it again: The devil trembles whenever he sees you on your knees. So, do not give him breathing space, bombard him every second and he will flee from you.

No panicking, no grumbling, no murmuring, no complaining, go down on your knees and fight. Learn to flow with the Holy Spirit for that is the secret of it all.

If I cannot learn from the twenty-six years of horror and sorrows of the life of my wonderful son Eloka Udem, who later went to be with the Lord; then I am fit to be stoned alive. That is why, if I am giving a message to someone who is nonchalant about it, I do not disturb myself. Why? Because I know that sooner or later the truth must show its face. If you cannot learn from your past experiences or from what happened to others, you are to be pitied.

WARRIORS ON THEIR KNEES

CHAPTER 1
THE WORD

The devil has been fighting against man for thousands of years and is an expert on warfare, especially spiritual warfare. He has some advantages over us.

He knows mankind and what tricks will work against man. He has observed behaviour for centuries since the creation and knows how to attack you successfully.

He knows God much better than any Christian in this world could ever know Him. He is not in fellowship with God, but he lived with God and observed the Triune Godhead for thousand years. Satan was in the presence of God all this time. Thus, he knows God very well. Again, he and his allies know the Bible very well, which is one of our main weapons. Many times during deliverance sessions, demons have quoted the Bible and they quoted it verbatim.

Beloved, those in the Dark Kingdom know how to organize and carry out their spiritual schemes against us. In fact, they are experts in spiritual warfare.

In contrast, you in the Church have been ignorant concerning their activities and how they operate. Due to this ignorance about the Dark Kingdom, your ability to wage successful spiritual warfare has been limited. Your ignorance has been bliss for Satan.

Honestly speaking, the Church has not effectively understood nor utilized the weapons at her disposal to fight a successful warfare. This is especially true concerning prayer and the Word. You have not properly understood how to use the Word, nor have you understood that there are different kinds of prayers in the Bible, each with a different purpose. Concerning the Word, read the following Scriptures:

"And take the helmet of salvation, and the sword of the Spirit, which is the Word of God." Ephesians 6:17

Beloved, it has not been understood in the Church and, it must be pointed out here that the Greek word in this verse Rhema - (meaning the spoken word.) is the Word of God (Rhema) that is coming out in contrast to logos (written word, the Bible) Often you have heard ministers or Christians hold their Bibles up and proclaim that it is their sword. This is not true.

Hear this, the Bible on your dining table at home is not your sword. The idea in Ephesians 6:17 is that the Word of God is used both offensively and to defend against the thrusts of the enemy. The Word cuts through the air and aims at the heart of Satan. But it must be emphasized that this is the spoken word and not the written word, the Bible. That is why the devil fights you so much when you attempt to study, memorize and meditate upon the Logos- word. The Word will have no power against him as long as you cannot speak it out of your mouth. You must take the Logos and make it a rhema of your confession against the Dark Kingdom. It is not the Bible that the devil fears, he already knows it word for word. He uses it against you the same way he did against Jesus and Job when he appeared before God as the accuser of the brethren.

Note that, it is the Bible coming out of mouth mixed

with faith to activate the Word that the devil and his cohorts fear. It is a tremendous force against the Dark Kingdom. Hence, the evil spirits will vehemently fight to prevent you from reading, meditating, memorizing, quoting, and appropriating the Logos Word to your life so that it becomes a thematic word against the Kingdom of Darkness.

Ignorance in this area is one reason why the Church is weak. There are some teachings in the Church called "confession principles" however, it has been opposed by many and taken to extremes by other groups.

Unfortunately, many have relegated confession to the teaching area of prosperity. This is probably because it is a popular topic to preach on and with which to obtain a large offering.

You must spend time reading and meditating on the Word yourself to allow the Holy Spirit instruct you. If you just take the Word of your Pastor, you may be in big trouble. You should learn the spiritual truths from the Bible and know the moving of the Holy Spirit in your own life. If not you will not know the will of God in your life and you will not be able to differentiate the truth from the false.

If you make out time to study the WORD of God and makeup time to be in His presence. As time goes on, you will eventually resemble the person you are spending time with. That is why it is said that " birds of the same feather flock together." Your final manifestation is greatly determined by whom you fellowship with.

As you live daily in the consciousness of God's present presence, the happenings around you will be such that will continually make you dance and praise the name of the Lord. Remember, grace is obtained in God's presence. He is the domain of grace, so for you to enjoy grace to the fullest, you must reside in His presence.

Hebrews 4:16 says: "Let us, therefore, come boldly to the throne of grace, that we may obtain mercy, and find grace in time of need."

Beloved, if you do not come into His presence, you will not obtain grace and mercy.

The power of the devil is increasing these days, do not be discouraged for the Word of God will meet all your needs. Every need you have or will ever have can be met from the Word. This is why the devil fights the Word and tries to distort it.

He knows the power of the Word. Listen carefully two things will keep you away from the promises of God, The two things are sin and unbelief. Satan operates on these to prevent God's blessings in your life.

Instead of praying about the problem pray the promises. Instead of praying about your worries, pray the Word. When the enemy creates a mess of this world in Genesis chapter one, God used words (the Spirit of His mouth) and brought the world back into order. Since you are created in the image of God and after the likeness of God, you too have the same power. (Genesis 1:26) It is the power of the spoken word that gives you life or death and releases blessings or curses.

You must effectively use anointed words to destroy the works of the enemy in your life, family and ministry. Replace all idle and ineffective words with anointed words.

The moment you start praying yokes will be destroyed, burdens will be lifted, and your life and those of your loved ones, will not be defeated.

God's Word is to be "a lamp for your feet, a light on your path" (Psalm 119: 105), it should certainly be a source of guidance for your prayer life. Consider a few of these passages, underline them in your Bible so that you can easily find them when you are looking for them.

Jesus taught you how to pray God's Word through His example when praying the "Lord's Prayer. (Matthew 6:9-13) Jesus used direct quotes from Scripture when He was tempted in the wilderness during His forty days and nights of fasting, He quoted Scripture.

Would you like your prayers to be more powerful? Pray the Scriptures. Hebrew 4:12 says that God's Word is alive and powerful, sharper than a two-edged sword. When you speak and pray the Scriptures, you are coming into an agreement with God and His power is released to answer your prayers.

1John 5:14, tells you that you can have confidence in God, not only does He hear your prayers, but He also promised to answer you when you pray in line with His will. He hastens to perform His Word'

Praying with the Word will increase your spiritual growth

Isaiah 54: 15, 17:

Behold, they shall surely gather together, but not by me: whosoever shall gather together against thee shall fall for thy sake.

No weapon that is formed against thee shall prosper, and every tongue that shall rise against thee in judgment thou shall condemn. This is the heritage of the servants of the LORD, and their righteousness is of me, saith the LORD.

These are some of the wonderful passages that can be used to guide your prayer life.

There is another way you can pray with the Word and I love it so much if somebody has been sending spiritual arrows to you and you know it is nothing but the truth. Just called the name of the person, ... and say, the Word of God said that" If I forgive you God will forgive me, but If I refuse to forgive you, God will not forgive me. So I forgive you for all the arrows you have been sending to me. I now hang a time bomb over your head that if you try it again, I am tying these scriptures to it:

1. Whosoever diggeth a pit will fall in it.

2. Whosoever breaks the hedge the serpent will bite.

3. Whosever rolls a stone; the stone will roll back to him.

So, no weapon fashioned against me shall prosper and any tongue that shall rise against me in judgment, I shall condemn.

Evil shall slay the wicked and those that hate the righteous shall be desolate.

CHAPTER 2
HEARING THE VOICE OF GOD

Beloved, it is the right of every child of God to hear the voice of the Lord himself. Every child of God ought to have direct access to the voice of the Father. Unfortunately, you are in the era where Christians chose to seek direction from Pastors, Apostles, and Prophets than from God.

Though, it is not bad to do that from genuine pastors that are spirit-filled. But now those "native doctors" in quote, handle the Bible and claim to be pastors, you are bound to fall into their traps. Regular practice of intimacy with the Lord will give you access to His glorious voice. The more consistent you are in giving Him undivided attention the more His voice will be clearer to you. Even the best prophet in town could fail, you that are led by the voice can be sure of standing aright.

Years back when I was going home, on the way, I decided to visit a sister living on the same street. As I was about to enter her house, I heard a voice, "Go home".

As I was climbing the stairs, I perceived smoky air, when I got to the door, it was open, so I entered. Oh my God! the parlour was full of thick black smoke. I just managed to trace where the smoke was coming from. I ran to the kitchen, behold a plastic gallon was burning _ very close to it was the gas cooker and the gas cylinder. I quickly carried water from the plastic containers in the passage and put off the fire.

When I checked there was nobody in the next room, for the house-help was downstairs. I rushed to the children's room, behold four of them were sleeping. I quickly woke them up and they left through the parlour.

Later, in the day, when I have fully recovered from what I saw, I prostrated before my Father and worshipped Him. If, God did not tell me to go home and if I did not hear the voice, I would have lost all. Pray seriously that you will always hear when God is speaking.

Close your eyes and pray that prayer now. Continue praying until you feel the presence of the Almighty around you.

One of my children when he was small loved to whisper, he would not like the next person in the room to hear him. He would come close and put his mouth on my ear and whisper. God do whisper too, and if you are not close to Him you will not hear Him. When He whispers and you are not attentive, you will not hear Him. Do not expect Him to thunder like thunder. Have you forgotten that He is the still small voice? For you to hear Him, you must drop all you are doing, move closer to Him and bend your ear over His head. If not, you will not hear the answer to your problem. Avoid distractions and noise and you will be in a better position to hear Him.

You cannot hear the still small voice from a distance, you have to draw closer my beloved. Remember, you must have an intimacy with God for you to hear His voice. Do you know that not everybody can discern the voice of the Lord?

I was repairing my tyre somewhere and after about twenty minutes, a man dressed as a mad man came to the dust bin and was searching for something in the bin.

All of a sudden four women very close to me started abusing the man. I did not understand why they were doing that, till I listened carefully and found out that they were accusing him of picking used sanitary pads from the bin.

I was angry in the Spirit, for I knew what that meant. So, I rebuked him and declared that whatever he had done with the ones he had collected be destroyed by the blood of Jesus Christ. As he was touching the bin, let the fire in the blood of Jesus Christ start burning him until he repents and stops working for the devil.

He stopped searching for the pads, turned and said, "Don't you know that I am from Saudi Arabia?"

I told him that he is from Saudi Arabia, but I am from above and that fire will continue to burn him until he repents. He muttered something we did not hear and ran away.

When I was about to leave, I heard a voice. “Go and alert somebody in the school."

The dust bin was by the side of a private school and ninety-nine percent of the sanitary pads must belong to innocent girls.

I pushed open the small gate and went into the school. I saw the Principal and narrated to her what happened. I also suggested that she should advise the girls to collect the pads for burning, for the days are evil.

If I did not hear from my Father, I would have gone home and those children will continue to suffer what they did not know. It is good to hear from God for directions and answers.

Learn to fill your mind with acts of God in the Bible times and His work in the present day. As you do this, your heart will be filled with adoration for Him. As you get into worship, you will hear His still small voice. Hearing God's voice is the highest point of fellowship with Him.

A sister dear to me thought that God has forgotten her by being nonchalant to her problems. She lamented profusely, one day God decided to address her. Listen attentively to her exact words:

"Praise the Lord. The road had been thorny and stony and no help from anybody, though brothers and sisters were there. I discovered that when you are passing through this wilderness experience, which is also a training and also not palatable, you tend to be alone. This is because it is taking you to the next level.

So that day, I had nothing with me, no job, no husband, no help, nothing at all, no companion. I was alone in the house, without knowing where to lean again. I have no food, the only coins available can only fetch me roasted corn at ESBS (Enugu State Broadcasting Service) which is very close to my house, where I cannot take transport to. So I collected the coins from the remaining change in my house and started trekking to ESBS to see if I can get roasted corn.

But before then, I had prayed in the morning, I came out in the sun so that I can have direct access to Heaven so that this God will hear me well. Because, if I stay inside, it will be blocking whatever... my utterances. After that prayer, I told Him, that He should kill me.

My mother has eight children, minus one, she can make

do with the other seven, instead of staying there and lamenting and regretting why I am existing. Because, to me, life is no longer of any value.

So, I went to get the corn, where I was standing in front of the corn seller a man.......said, " Sister, who are you?"

I said, as usual, my name is Ogo.

He said, " And you are asking God to kill you?"

"You are asking God to kill you with all these deposits in you, you want to go back with them?"

"Look, He is the one that sent me to you, listen and listen very well.

"Do not say that kind of prayer you said in the morning, before you incur the wrath of the LORD. He is the one that sent me to you. I repeat, never you pray that type of prayer again to Him. You have heard me very well.

"Don't you know that you are a vessel? You want to go back without releasing all those deposits in you. No, my dear. You cannot pray......and He will not allow it. Go back it will be well."

At that juncture, I did not remember whether I paid for the corn or not, and I did not know how the man disappeared. I took off my shoes to start running back to the house. As soon as possible, I zoomed off to the house.

Beloved, you have heard it all, desist from blaming God. If God did not send that man to her, who knows what would have happened to the sister? Thank God that now the sister is bubbling in the Lord.

Hearing the voice of God is good, excellent, marvellous, and beneficial. But, will you be able to do it without giving a damn? Sometimes, what He will tell you to do will make people look at you as if are wearing the back of your cloth. Some will see you as a wicked and stupid fellow.

Follow me to 1King 13:9-10

"For so was it charged me by the Word of the LORD, saying, "Eat no bread, nor drink water, nor turn again by the same way that thou cometh"

So he went another way, and returned not by the way that he came to Bethel."

This young Prophet obeyed and was going home when the old prophet (11-23) sent his sons to bring him back. He came back and disobey God by eating with the old prophet.

Listen to verse 24.

"And when he was going, a lion met him by the way, and slew him; and his carcass was cast in the way, and the ass stood by it, the lion also stood by the carcass."

Beloved, why did the lion not hear the prophet? Why did it not attack the ass either? See what the old prophet said about the prophet he had deceived.

Verse 26...It is the man of God, who was disobedient unto the Word of the LORD: therefore, the LORD hath delivered him unto the lion which hath torn him and slain him according to the Word of the LORD, which he spake unto him."

You see, the very prophet that deceived him was the one that broadcast that he was disobedient. Learn and be very careful.

In my book," SUBMISSION NOT OPTIONAL" I narrated what happened in November 2013, when my wonderful and cherished son died. The LORD told me to leave with the siblings after a few hours of the burial in the village. I obeyed and ignored what people were saying because I did not want to disobey my DADDY.

Will you be able to close your ears? Will you be able to stand on your feet, while tongues wag? Will you damn the consequence and look up to Heaven?

Dear, it is easier said than done. There are other things I have done and people talked and talked, but I was not moved, because I am sure of what I heard. I can never mock my DADDY and dance to the tune of mortal man.

A sister narrated to me what a nurse told her: there was no money to buy JAMB (Joint Matriculation Admission Board) form for her sister and their uncle told her to come for the money. She collected the money, bought the form, and did very well. But when she went to check her score she could not believe what she saw.

This continued, till the fourth time and it was ministered to the nurse to give her sister her money and keep that of the uncle. Her money was used to buy the JAMB form and this time around she was successful. She said their uncle did not believe what he heard and from that, they learnt something.

The lady graduated from LUTH (Lagos University Teaching Hospital Lagos) with flying colours. Why are you so blunt about what is above you? Why do you doubt things without trying to prove them?

It is also the experience some people have with weddings and burial money. A lot of people complain that money is usually useless, and they were not able to do something tangible with it.

Yes, the Bible told us that the days are evil, whether you believe it or not, that is the Word of God. There is nothing people cannot do because the devil had seared their hearts. Some people lay curses on the money, some keep it in their evil temples for days or weeks before giving them out.

So the moment you collect such money, do not use it, deposit it in a bank and exchange it. So that by the time they will be calling back the money, it will no longer be with you. For that, whatever they have projected to the money will never affect you.

Beloved, hearing from God cannot be overemphasized, a pastor friend was narrating to us what happened to some people travelling on a bus.

When they were travelling and the bus stopped to do something, these two guys went down and started fighting heavily. After separating them, in a twinkle of an eye they will rush each other and start fighting again.

This continued and people were confused about why they should be behaving like that. God opened the eyes of someone inside the bus and he said that anytime you separate them, something will just blow fuuu... and they will rush again and start fighting.

Anytime they are separated, that thing will come again, this time one of them brought a bottle and the voice shouted to the man on the bus, "Are you watching and you do not want to save them?

Then the voice shouted at the man, "Do something, you are there, watching them kill themselves."

The man then shouted, "I rebuke you in the name of Jesus."

My dear, the two stopped fighting immediately and grabbed each other smiling. Each one called the name of the other, and said, why are we fighting? They jumped into the bus and the journey continued.

If you fail to get something out of this, it means you are still sleeping. Wake up and see what is happening around you.

These days, our youth mistakenly believe that they can keep Almighty God outside their lives and still succeed in life. How impossible! Trace your way back to God and reconcile with Him.

Someone was telling me how all the weddings he attended the previous year, had all suffered massive setbacks and ugly conflicts; despite the enormous cost and lavish nature of these weddings. Strangely, the concerned parties all had nothing reasonable to blame for the state of their marriages.

Indeed, the days are evil and one needs to give God the front-seat in every decision making, else pain and regret will be the result of hasty unguided decisions.

CHAPTER 3
THE BLOOD

The holiness of the life which you are trusting God for does not undermine the Blood provision. The Blood provision is not only for the weak alone, it is for anybody human. It is not for you because you have been falling into sin, it is because it is only under the blood covenant that you can have a relationship and fellowship with God.

The Blood was also provided as a weapon to silence the accuser of the Brethren. It is a powerful spiritual weapon that most Churches have forgotten about. The Bible tells us that the life of every single creature is in the blood. You should realize that the devil is interested in making you sin because it allows him to attack you. It gives him the weapon to accuse you, it is the only thing that strengthens him to oppress you.

So what does the blood do? The Blood of Jesus blocks all effects of sin that you have committed and renders the devil empty-handed. So he has nothing again with which to plead his case against you.

I want you to appreciate the power of that first provision – the Blood. Follow me to Colossians 2: 14-15.

Blotting out the handwriting of ordinances that was contrary to us, and took it out of the way, nailing it to his cross.

And having spoiled principalities and powers, he made a

show of them openly, triumphing over them in it.

The devil will lure you and push you to sin, then he will quickly open up his register and say, "In the year 2015, sister.....told lies when she was giving testimony-noted. Then he will push you again to gossip about another sister. You will not know, just out of envy you said things you know we're not true.

The devil will quickly bring his register, on September 20th 2015 still, sister .... told lies when she was giving testimony and all liars will go to hell according to the Scripture. He keeps all the commandments you have disobeyed, for he has a very cumulative record of all your sins.

Remember, he is the one that tempted you, but quickly grabs it and put it down. What does he need it for? Even though you have repented, he will keep quiet, but the day you are looking for something serious from God. You will see the devil and he will just start flashing those things. He will start opening his pages.

Take, for instance, there is something you are asking God for, as you start praying the devil will be reminding you of all those things and then bring you to the position of condemnation. Truly speaking, you are not going to get those things. Many a time, you will say you are praying, but dear you are not praying, you are listening to the accusations the devil is flashing to you.

Sin constitutes a list in the hand of the devil, he does not use it every time. He only uses it when he wants to deal with you and he will just draw it out from the archives. He is used to doing that, and he accuses our brethren day and night before the Lord.

So how do you overcome him? It is only by the Blood of the Lamb. God provided the Blood to silence the accuser. Remember the scripture said God blotted out all the ordinances, all the accusations from the devil. The Blood of Jesus comes to blot them out.

Beloved, when next the devil comes, Jesus will tell him to provide his evidence and when he opens the archives, he will see a blank page.

"So what reason do you have to stand against my child," Jesus will ask.

"But, I have a reason."

The Lord will tell him to present his evidence, and then will he realize that it had been blotted out. From that moment he loses the power to accuse.

God knows that the devil will never allow you to rest, so he makes the Blood provision. The provision carries you to a point where not only your sin is forgiven, but you also come to the place of sanctification under the cover of the Blood.

Grace does not condone sin, but the Blood creates a cover so that the sin question can be dealt with in the presence of God.

This provision must be constant, must be progressive, you must work under it every day. When you wake up in the morning you plead the Blood and sing:

Oh the Blood of Jesus 2x

Oh the Blood of Jesus

The Blood was shed for me.

The Lord will say. "Welcome my child, not because you are now what He wants you to be, but there is an interface of the Blood that allows Him to still touch you." He touches you through the Blood to perfect the cleansing and the washing of water by the Word of God.

Stop now for a while, and start thanking God for the Blood. Thank Him for the efficacy of the Blood. Thank Him for the provision of the Blood. Thank Him for the Blood that speaks better things than the blood of Abel. Thank the Lord for the Blood. Thank Jesus for the Blood. Thank Him, for when He sees the blood he will pass over you.

CHAPTER 4
SPEAKING IN TONGUE

Unlike the other prayers, references to this particular prayer are found in the New Testament. It is because this type of prayer did not occur until after the Holy Spirit was poured out on the day of Pentecost.

From Jude 20: "But ye, being, building up yourselves on your most holy faith, praying in the Holy Ghost."

As you know that praying in the Spirit is prayer in other tongues. When you receive the Baptism of power you receive the ability to speak, sing and eventually think in other tongues.

This is quite different from all other prayers, the prayer comes from your spirit and through this prayer, you can pray the "perfect will of God."

See what is written in Romans 8:26.

"Likewise the Spirit also helpeth our infirmities for we know not what we should pray for as we ought: But the Spirit itself maketh intercession for us with groanings which cannot be uttered.

If you can pray the perfect will of God over a person or a situation, that becomes the most powerful of all prayers. You can pray the perfect will of God because the Holy Spirit is praying through you. He is using your body and voice as a vessel for prayer. In this type of prayer, the Holy Spirit is doing the prayer because He is the one that gives the words you pray. In case you become more spiritually minded, your discernment increases and you can hear the voice of God better.

You are bound to groan for hours in the Spirit as you progress in speaking in tongues. You can groan for a lost soul or someone in trouble and later you see God answering your petitions.

Remember that this happens after you have gotten your salvation, the Holy Spirit then fills you with His Spirit. When you are filled with the Holy Spirit, the Spirit then gives you a very personal language - that is speaking in tongues. It is just a gift of speaking in other tongues.

When the 12 disciples of Jesus Christ received the Baptism of the Holy Spirit in the Upper Room on the day of Pentecost, they spoke in different tongues.

Personally, when my gratitude towards God overflows and I cannot express my thanksgiving enough in my language, I speak in tongues. In doing that my spirit becomes refreshed. Again, when the heaviness and sorrows are on my way, I normally burst into tongue.

When you have no specific prayer point, you may also pray to God in tongues, since the Spirit will be praying through you. Also, during a personal night vigil, you can pray in tongues to enable you to pray freely for a longer time.

Praying in tongues is not human thought arranged, it is Holy Ghost's prayer. The Holy Spirit uses your voice and your spirit as we have earlier mentioned.

Praying in tongues does not place a mental burden on you,

for if you pray for a long time in tongues, you will not be tired.

It is good to speak in tongues, for you are drawn closer to God, and when you are closer to God, He shares His secrets with you.

When you feel that God is not near, speak in tongues and you will experience the closeness of His presence surrounding you.

Some people have the grace of interpreting their tongues while praying. So you should pray that you will be able to understand what the Spirit had spoken.

Praying in tongues can be a sign to unbelievers that God is with you.

1Corinthians 14:22 says "Wherefore tongues are for sign, not to them that believe, but to them that believe not." It also gives you great refreshment and rest in your soul.

To you that live in a world of stressful affliction, praying in tongues gives you refreshment. When you are weary and your heart is full of pain, praying in tongues helps you to receive restoration.

Since you are living in a world limited by time and space, you do not always know the dangers of your circumstances or accidents that could befall you beforehand. So when you pray in tongues, the Holy Spirit delivers you from unknown dangers and enables you to overcome the sufferings of life.

Beloved, praying brings you into a deeper grace of God's loving care. It is a blessing of God that helps your shortcomings in prayer. So, seeking to be filled with the

Holy Spirit and receiving the gift of speaking in other tongues is very right.

Praying in tongues helps you break the strongholds of the devil and live victoriously. For you as a Christian, the number one priority is prayer! The number two priority is prayer! Number three is prayer! And number four is PRAYER. Nothing else my beloved.

Pray always so that your heavenly Father's will, will be done forever.

There is something I noticed when you make speaking in tongues your lifestyle:

1. Bitterness can never be comfortable in your heart.

2. The spirit of anger is

3. The problem of forgetting your dreams the moment you open your eyes, will be minimal.

Praying in tongues promotes growth, it improves you and strategically sets you up for greater glory. Activate the function of the Holy Spirit you want to manifest in your life by constant speaking in tongues.

When you are down or tired, if you pray in the Spirit long enough, you will find the required strength to understand the assignment ahead of you. Every assignment that God has for you is First spiritual and then physical. This is why you cannot effectively perform a divine assignment using only physical aspects of a divine assignment, you need spiritual stamina or input to be effective.

CHAPTER 5
PRAISE AND WORSHIP

Praise according to Webster's dictionary, means to extol, laud, honour, acclaim, express approval. To praise then is to give positive affirmation, expressing your approval of something. Giving your approval means that you accept or agree with what you approve of. So to praise God for a difficult situation, sickness or disaster, means literally that you accept and approve of its happening, as part of God's plan for your life.

You cannot praise God without being thankful for the thing you are praising Him for. And you cannot be thankful without being happy about whatever you are thankful for. Praising, then involves both gratitude and joy.

The very fact that you praise God and not some unknown fate also means that you are accepting the fact that God is responsible for what is happening. Otherwise, it would make little sense to thank Him for it.

Always be joyful. Always keep on praying. No matter what happens, always be thankful, for this is God's will for you who belongs to Christ Jesus. 1 Thessalonians 5:16-18.

If you can praise God for your circumstance, simply because you accept the Word of the Bible that you are supposed to praise God in everything. Praising Him, you may soon experience the results of an attitude of consistent thanksgiving and joy, and in turn, your faith is strengthened and you can continue to live that way.

Beloved, are you surrounded by difficult circumstances right now? Have you been struggling to understand why they have come to you? Then try to accept with your understanding that God loves you and has allowed those circumstances because He knows they are good for you. Praise Him for what He has brought into your life; do it deliberately and with your understanding.

Since you have nothing to lose in praising God, why don't you try it? You should understand that praising God is not a patent medicine, neither a cure-all nor a magic formula for success. It is a way of life that is solidly backed up in God's Word. You praise God, not for the expected results but the situation just as it is.

Praise is based on a total and joyful acceptance of the present as part of God's loving and perfect will for you.

Praise is not based on what you think or hope will happen in future. You praise God, not for what you expect will happen around you, but you praise Him for what He is and where you are right now.

God has a perfect plan for your life, you may look at the circumstances surrounding you and think you have been standing still forever on one painful spot. The more you pray and cry to God to help you, the more the circumstances seem to pile up. The turning point cannot come until you begin to praise God for your situation instead of crying for Him to take it all away.

The turning point in your life comes when you begin to accept your present circumstances with thanksgiving. God has a perfect plan for your life, but He cannot move you to the next level of His plan until you joyfully accept your present situation as part of that plan. What happens next is God's move, not yours.

A changed attitude brings changed circumstances, when you stop complaining and start smiling, you feel different; then others will treat you differently and your whole life can undergo a dramatic change for the best. For instance, if you smile, the world will smile with you, but when you cry, you cry alone. God wants you to thank Him for everything that has brought you to Him.

I use to do what I called Holy Ghost School after I will explain that to you. For quite some time I stopped, but God used a Pastor friend of mine to warn me about depression and anger. That notwithstanding, God personally warned me and told me not to be sad. I recollected myself and decided to go back to Holy Ghost School. I also decided to go back to my usual way of praising and thanking God in all situations instead of grumbling.

On the third day precisely, as I was running to enter my jeep, I slipped and fell – one leg in front, the other one at the back. I managed to get up and saw that my legs were not broken, but I have bruises on my left leg.

I said, "God, I thank you for this fall, thank you that I did not break my leg. Thank you that if this did not happen something worse than this would have happened."

Barely forty-five minutes when I got home, as I was going inside my android phone slipped from my hand and fell. The screen cracked – I mean real cracking, but it was still working. I said, "God thank you that my phone fell and the screen cracked, if this did not happen maybe something worse than this would have happened.

Then it dawned on me that I have gotten the secret again. I did not grumble, I did not get angry and talked like a madwoman. I then realized in my spirit that by the grace of God I have bitten the enemy below the belt and he is not happy that I have at last jumped out of the valley of depression.

What am I trying to say – if you learn to praise God in all situations you have gotten the secret and the enemy will cancel your name from his evil list. Why? He now knows that he can no longer pin you down with depression and sadness.

Sincere prayers are the door for God's power to move into your life. But the prayer of praise releases more of God's power than any other form of a petition. The Holy Bible has examples demonstrating this fact.

"But thou art holy, O thou that inhabitest the praise of Israel." (Psalm 22:3)

No wonder God's power and presence are near when you praise Him. He dwells, inhabits, resides, in your praises.

Check 2 Chronicle 20 and you will see a remarkable example of how God works while you praise Him.

Jehoshaphat the king of Judah, discovered that his little kingdom was surrounded by the powerful armies of his enemies – the Moabites, the Ammonites. He knew that he could not fight them, so he went to God with praises and the enemies fought against themselves.

An important step in the act of praising God is to take away your eyes from the threatening circumstances and look to

God instead. Notice that Jehoshaphat was not just closing his eyes to the threat against his kingdom or pretending the enemies were not there. He took careful stock of the situation, recognized his helplessness, and turned to God for help.

You are not to be blind to the very real threats of evil in your life. Seeing them for what they only give your greater cause to praise and thank God for working in them with perfect control and authority. But you are not to be preoccupied with the appearance of evil around you. See it, admit your helplessness to cope with it in your strength. Then turn to God.

You do not have the power to deal with the circumstances of your life, so obviously, the battle is not yours but God's.

When Jesus was confronted with the death of Lazarus, He prayed a simple prayer of thanksgiving. When the stone was rolled away from the grave opening where Lazarus had been buried for four days. Jesus lifted His and said, "Father, thank you for hearing me." (John 11:41). Then He commanded Lazarus to come from the grave, and the man who had been dead for four days walked out.

Praise is an active response to what God has done and is doing for you in your life and this world through His Son Jesus Christ and the person of the Holy Spirit. If you doubt your heart what God has done and is doing, you cannot wholeheartedly praise Him. Uncertainty about the Good News will always be a barrier to praise. If you want to be able to praise God in everything, you need to be sure your foundation is solid and without cracks of doubt and uncertainty.

Beloved, God is love, everything He does is love in action. Your problem is that you have such a limited picture of what love is all about. You have been hurt and disappointed by human love, the kind that rewards you and accepts you when you are good and punishes and rejects you when you are bad. But that is not like God's love at all.

As you praise and thank God for all that has happened in your life, you tend to build up your faith in the Lord. You should always remember that the Bible tells you that you can be saved by faith, healed by faith, justified by faith, shielded by faith, walk in faith, stand in faith, live by faith, and inherit the promises of God by faith. Always praise God, when you have a wonderful experience of His presence; but do not let your faith depend on how you feel.

I needed four tyres at once for my jeep due to the bad roads in our country, then on Sunday I prayed telling God that before Friday He will give me four tyres. How He will do it, I do not know, I praise and worship Him. I had the money for just one tyre, on Wednesday I went to my Mechanic to help me buy a good one. We were there when I got an alert on my phone – naira worth 50 dollars, instead of buying one I ended up buying three. Then the following day being Thursday, God provided money for the fourth tyre; What an awesomely awesome God we serve! If He did it for me, He will also do more for you.

Just forget the problems, stop seeing how big they are, just believe you have a big God. It is not your business how He is going to solve it, neither is it your business whom He is going to use in solving the problem. Just look above, for help only comes from above.

It did not end there, I opened my mouth wide and testified

to everybody I saw on my way. I even had to phone some loved ones telling them what the Lord had done for me. I remembered one of them told me his friend also had four of his tyres bad and he had planned to be buying one every month and so he parked his car.

The Lord wants me to tell everyone who will listen to be thankful for every detail of their lives, and He will open the windows of heaven and pour out more goodness than they can ever ask for or hope for.

Remember, you cannot deserve God's blessings. You cannot work for them or earn them. He gives everything to you as a gift, and because of His goodness. You must learn to understand and accept that.

God does His things at the appointed time or the fullness of time. He is never slow or late. He is never one minute late.

Praise God in all circumstances whether they seem good or bad to you; trust that God is using them to unfold His wonderful plan for your life.

CHAPTER 6
GRATITUDE

Beloved, you can move God to do more for you, through the heart of gratitude.

What is gratitude? It is the state of being grateful, and the synonyms are appreciation, thankfullness and peacefulness.

If you show gratitude to God, you are bound to achieve great things in your life.

In 1Kings 3: 3 - 15, King Solomon showed his gratitude to God. He remembered all the intrigues and battles that led to his emergence as king, and He was moved to give thanks.

King David was so grateful to God that he expressed it in his dance, to the point that he was disdained by his wife Michal. (2 Samuel 6:16) He forgot he was a king, because he was happily demonstrating his gratitude to his Maker. If you really have a heart of gratitude to God, when things are working, you will praise God and when things are not going in the direction you expect, you still praise Him. Why? You know fully well that the faithfulness of God will never allow you to suffer loss.

Are you surrounded by uncountable enemies? Do not be troubled. Just trust in the Lord, and you will definitely see His salvation. Are you passing through the storms of life? Put your trust in God, and bless the Name of thc Lord.

Always remember that the prayer of gratitude is normally addressed to God and not to the situation you want to change. The Lord in Heaven has been so good to you, He had never ceased to be faithful and kind to you. If it had not been for the Lord on your side, the devil would have finished you. For these reasons and many more, you need to make thanksgiving your lifestyle.

Thanksgiving is an indispensable activity for every child of God. For your life to experience the blessings of God on a continuous basis, you need to thank Him always. Stop complaining, look around you and you will definitely see the goodness of the Lord.

A lifestyle of thanksgiving can make a lot of difference in your life within a very short time. Through thanksgiving your lost glorious can be restored.

Thanksgiving is the door that ushers you into God's blessings, and it is not something you do in a hurry. You must take your time and do it well, because God also takes His time as He blesses you with innumerable miracles. There are blessings reserved for those who thank the Lord. He will always launch them to the realm of unimaginable favour.

Your thanksgiving will only be acceptable if it comes from a heart of worship and for you to worship God in truth, you must live in a holy life.

Follow me to Colossians 1:12-13:

"Giving thanks unto the Father, which hath made us meet to be caretakers of inheritance of the Saints in light: who hath delivered us from the power of darkness, and hath translated us into the kingdom of His dear Son"

In prayer of Gratitude (thanksgiving) you simply give thanks to God for all He has done for you. It is good to do that, for your giving thanks is a demonstration of your faith that God has answered your prayers. It is also very effective when used as prayer of faith or prayer of petition. God is like our earthly parents, He enjoys us coming to Him with thanks, instead of always coming to Him with shopping list.

If you are regretting your past, remember, God is looking at your future. His love for you is not based on your performance or your virtues. He loved you while you were yet a sinner. Rom 5:5-8

Change your thinking, you do not have more probably than other people - you just think about them more often. It is what you think that produces how you feel. To experience a feeling, you must first have the thought that produces it.

So what will you do? Change how you think and you will change how you feel. Nothing can hold your negative feelings in place, other than your own thinking. Next time you are feeling upset check your thinking - it will be negative. It is always that way. The truth is, it is your thinking that is negative, not your life. Once you understand that, you are back on the path towards happiness again.

But change takes time; you did not become negative overnight and you will not necessarily be positive overnight either. But you can earnestly start now. How? Start treating your negative thoughts, the same way you will treat flies in a gathering - push them away and replace them with thoughts that are excellent or praise worthy

We fail because of negative outlook. Do not create negative atmosphere, your words create the climate you live in. You feel free yourself from anxiety by thanksgiving - not by complaining. Never let the level of your thanksgiving be according to your circumstances for God is greater than any circumstance.

If You have always been negative, do not expect to change overnight. Make a start, from now on if you cannot say something helpful, say nothing.

Begin to look for what is good and you will find it.

"Whatever is true... noble.. right.. pure.. lovely.. think about such things" Philippians 4:8.

You fail because you are in the wrong place. Before you start the journey, check the road map. Ask God for direction. His promise is all.

"In all thy ways acknowledge Him and He shall direct thy paths". Proverbs 3:6. God has a plan and a purpose for your life.

You fail because of your inability or unwillingness to change. Change can be painful, especially if you have been doing things a certain way for a longtime.

Words paint pictures. You need to see it as well as hear it. Remember, experience is not what happens to you, it is what you do with what happens to you.

CHAPTER 7
NIGHT WATCH

I love Night Watch so much, it has done wonders in my life. It is also known as Night Vigil, and I always remember that Psalm 144:1-2 records the prayer of a skilled warrior by name David. From his days as a Shepherd boy and through out his days as king of the nation of Isreal, God empowered him in the art, technologies of strategic prayer and spiritual warfare.

His skill and expertise were gained as God in His sovereignty placed him in the midst of a variety of battles ranging from encounters with bears and lions, to His confrontation with Goliath and lastly the battle he fought with His son Absalom.

In this Psalm, David made us to know that it was only Jehovah Gibbor, the Mighty Man of War, who taught him warfare strategies and tactics. He provided the divine empowerment for success.

He declares, "Blessed be the LORD, my Strength which teachers my hands to war, and my fingers to fight. My goodness and my fortress; my high tower, and my deliverer; my shield, and He in whom I trust; who subdued my people under me."

From the life experiences of David, I have learnt that the only way you can become a skilful warrior is to be trained and placed in the midst of a battle. It is only when you are placed in the furnace of afflictions and when all he'll break loose around you that you can truly be trained in the art of strategic prayer and spiritual warfare. It is only perfect practice that makes perfect.

You do not get the level of training you need to become an effective prayer warrior by playing war games. You have got to face a real enemy on a real battle field. It is only when my DADDY trains you in the midst of an actual battle that you gain true experience.

Beloved, simply reading the Bible or attending workshops, seminars and conferences will not turn you into an effective warrior. Always remember that it is only when you are placed in the middle of a battle, or when there is no one or nothing to save you but God that a true "warrior" is born.

Always remember that your times of struggle, testing and temptation are divine opportunities to be trained in the art of strategic prayer and spiritual warfare. All these are authentic training grounds God has chosen to bring you into true dominion. Did the Bible not tell us to "pray and not faint" ?(Luke 18:1)

Beloved, do you know why I love Night Watch so much? The moment, I discovered the joy and efficacy of doing it outside, I never stopped looking forward to it every day. Unless, I am so tired or I am outside the city.

During Night Watch outside, everywhere is calm, you feel the breeze, and behold the firmament. You can look up to your Daddy, spreading your hands and worshipping Him with awesome worship songs. This can last for hours without getting tired, you can also kneel down or prostrate before your Father. From worship you can enter into tongues while marching round the house or dancing round the house.

You can start bombarding the enemy with the WORD of God in your heart:

"No weapon fashioned against you shall prosper....

"I am more than conqueror....

"Evil shall slay the wicked and those that hate the righteous shall be desolate. (Psalm 34:21)

"I overcome by the Blood of the Lamb and the words of my testimony"

You can burst into tongues again, but this time with anger to restore all the enemy had taken away from you. Finally, you can end with thanksgiving and plead the Blood of Jesus Christ all over the place. Beloved, before you know it you must have spent not less than three hours outside with ease.

While some people encounter God and ask for nothing, some ask for crumbs while few ask for big things. Again while some are ready to wait until their desires are granted, some are desperate.

Even though God has the ability to do all things, how fast your desires will be granted is often determined by your level of desperation. Desperate people do desperate things to get results, and so the attitude of their prayer is usually different from that of those who can wait

In Mark 2:1-5, the friends of the paralysed man, could not take it any longer, so they opened the roof and lowered their friend before Jesus. Lord Jesus had to suspend everything and attend to him.

How desperate are you to receive your miracle? If you say you are desperate, where are the signs of your desperation? Desperate people break protocol! They refuse to wait where others are waiting and try out new measures that others may never think of.

Desperate people refuse to be limited by what limits others, and they will do everything possible to get the result they desire.

When God sees desperate faith in action, He will never turn it down. If you are not desperate, you will definitely be placed at the end of the line. If you are a bit violent, you can end up in the middle of the queue. But if you are truly desperate, you will be moved to the front, irrespective of how long others have waited to get there.

Desperate people are persistent. They draw attention of other people in their bid to get what they desire. Although, desperate people can be a nuisance, they do not care about who they inconvenience as long as they get what they want.

I ask again, "how desperate are you for divine intervention over your situation? Cry out to God now and let Him hear the desperation in your voice and see it in your actions. He will surely answer you.

Lastly, listen to the advice given from a father (who has served the devil for a while) to his daughter who was supposed to take over from him as the priest of a Shrine.

While he was describing the order of rites and services to

his daughter; the father listed out three categories of people and cautioned his daughter to avoid and fear them greatly:

1. People that pray in the night (Night Prayer)
2. People with a steady praying habit even while driving or walking (intermittent praying).
3. People who pray lengthy prayers (spend long hours in prayer).

Stop grumbling and murmuring, stop crying and lamenting, turn your cares into prayers. Do you not know that when the world pushes you to your knees you are in perfect position to pray. Shalom!

CHAPTER 8
DREAMS

Beloved do not joke with your dreams, for they may reveal many things about your life. Monitor them and make them your pray points.

Some say that they do not dream at all, but I am of the opinion that they dream, but the moment they open their eyes the enemy wipes them away from their memory. It is a demonic oppression of the enemy. I personally experience such, but when that happens I am really mad at the enemy. At times when reading the Bible in the morning I will remember some of them or part of them.

Have you forgotten Joseph the dreamer? In Genesis 37:5-10 He dreamt that he was binding shelves with His brothers in the field and lo, his sheaf arose and stood upright, while those of brothers made obeisance to his sheaf.

Again he dreamt that the sun, the moon and the eleven stars bowed to Him. His brethren envied him but his wise father observed the saying.

Though, the hatred made them to sell him to the Ishmealites; he later became what he saw in the dream.

Anyway, you should learn from the life of Joseph and be careful when you tell your dreams. Some dreams are so real that they materialize in few days, some may happen exactly the way you see it, while some may be opposite.

Monitor your dreams to know exactly how they operate and check the trend of events in your life.

CHAPTER 9
SEED SOWING

Beloved, follow me to 2 Corinthians 9:10 to see what is written there.

"No he that ministereth seed to the shower both minister bread for your food, and multiply your seed, and increase the fruits of your righteousness.

Now you know that you are a co-labourer with God, you definitely have a divine colouring. Your life is dedicated y your sowing in every sense. You will never miss your harvest when you understand this very well. Only those who are addicted to sowing are working on their harvests, became God does not release what is in His hand until what is in your hand is released. Do you not know that your seed is the breakthrough you are looking for?

When you are an addicted seed shower, you are following God with faith attitude to release your harvest. Life can be compared to bike riding, where you keep your balance by moving ahead - this moving ahead is done by sowing.

Your level of sowing dictates your harvest - whether super or lean. Every seed has the power of abundance inside and so when it explodes, it produces a harvest. No short cut, you either follow the principle or you forfeit all. It is now that you prepare what you will be in future.

Beloved, examine now if you are really living by the seed principle. God said, give and it shall be given unto you. That means that the moment you give you must get something back. Life is much better for you the moment you start living by seed principle. All you need is obedience and you will see a great harvest.

Make a decision now, to stay connected with the harvest God has for you. Remember, the birds cannot fly with only one wing, so will you never collect anything without giving out. For you to get to your destination safe, you must obey God's instructions. You either cooperate with God or you cooperate with Satan. God has everything in your harvest account, the ATM card is your seed.

Many people eat their seeds as their bread and so end in lack. When you understand the principle of these things, it will help you to secure a better future. Is it possible to eat your cake and have it? I will like you to answer. Your actions are what determine where you are heading to, and they are nothing but your seed.

When God gives seed to the shower, it is connected to the harvest. There are great things you have not been able to achieve just because you have not sown the seeds of actions to make them manifest. Do you not realize that sowing seed is doing what is necessary and possible through which the possible can be achieved? Stop copying others for you are not a copycat, again do you not know that we all have different question papers before us to answer? We are not studying the same course my beloved. Keep on sowing, never stop on the way so that you will achieve your purpose.

Learn to wait patiently for your action seeds to grow. Also sow your life to affect others for that is how life becomes meaningful to you. If you can focus on your seeds, you will never miss your harvests. Be very careful of the seed you use, for they speak for you even when you are gone.

When you sow seeds, God is working things out for you even when it does not look so, and great miracles will come out where you least expect. Keep your faith and patience, for God's trimming is perfect. God might not be early but definitely He will never be late. Look to Him with patience and true faith and heaven will soon announce you.

More often than not we associate sowing with giving of money; for this reason, some people who do not have money believe that they do not t anything to sow. If you do not have money you can sow your talent into the work of the kingdom. It can be through praying, using your talents or your skills, there is no one who has nothing to sow. You can use your gift in drama to entertain the kingdom and draw them nearer to God. Everyone has something to sow, all you never to do is to identify what you have. (Romans 22:6-8)

The seed you sow will never leave your life. It simply moves from where you are today, to where you will be tomorrow, but when you get there it will no longer be the seed you planted, but the harvest you need. As long as you keep sowing, you will keep on reaping.

God will never ask you for something you do not have, He will ask you for something you will like to keep

You always have enough to create what you need. When what you have is not enough, just make it a seed. The moment you put that seed in God's hand, your next harvest begins.

Life is a series of outcomes, sometimes the outcome is

what you want. Great! Figure out what you did right, and keep doing it. Sometimes the outcome is what you never expected. Great too. Figure out what you did wrong and do not do it again. Because some people do not act, they do not gain experience.

Until you quit making excuses and accept personal responsibility for your life - nothing will change. No matter how often you fall down, you are not a failure until you blame somebody else for pushing you down.

When are you going to stop blaming others? look in the mirror and say. "I am responsible for my life, and nobody else.

You may smile, but as long as you keep blaming others and refusing to accept responsibility for yourself, you will never discover how great your life could have been.

When you sow a seed in tears, you will reap its yield in joy. Moreover, what you reap will be determined by what you have sown. If you want to sow a seed, pray fervently and the Holy Spirit will show you where to sow it. For if you sow in a desert you are bound to get nothing.

Beloved, if you pray and pray and nothing seem to be working. You cry and cry and nobody seemed to be moved, then sow a seed and many doors will open.

CHAPTER 10
MEDITATION

The most powerful gift of God to man, is MEDITATION. 1Timothy 4:16, says:

"Meditate upon these things; give thyself wholly to them; that they profiting May appear to all."

As you meditate on the scriptures, you have read, you establish their manifestation in your life. Remember, God told Joshua:

"This book of the law shall not depart out of thy mouth, but thou shall meditate there in day and night, that thou mayest observe to do according to all that is written therein for then they shall make their way prosperous, and then thou shall have good success." (Joshua 1:8)

Listen very careful, you will not make your way PROSPEROUS. LIFE IS NOT OPTIONAL, you cannot be prosperous until you have read the "BOOK." It is also the BOOK of His Law and Status. It is the BIBLE. You cannot have a good success until you read this book and meditate on it. You do not read it and put it away, rather you read it and study it. It must be your conversation and declaration. Whenever you open your mouth, that is what should be coming out from your mouth. Each time you close your mouth, it should be that the word is being chewed and eaten in your heart. It must be the subject of every discussion in your life.

It shall not depart from your mouth. There is nothing important you are talking about, if it is not this Book of the Law. It must be on your lips at every point in time. It must be in your mouth in every discussion.

Everything you do must find its relevance in the WORD. Your actions must be the respect of the prescription in this Book.

Beloved, God's emphasis that the word must abide in your heart is clear. You must make it your language for heaven and earth will pass away, but this WORD must be fulfilled!

This book must be read always and it must be your daily companion in everything. During the day, the night, turbulent day of work, it must be the thoughts continually and must be your quiet meditation.

Use that time of murmuring, grumbling and borrowing to meditate on the WORD. Fill your heart all the time with the WORD. Dig deep into it day and night, not only during fellowship and devotion.

Scripture is the comprehensive wisdom of God concerning every aspect of your life. It has an answer to every question in your heart and it also provides every economic solution to your needs in life.

Bible is the book written by God and it is the only BLUE PRINT He had given for every problem. It contains the genesis of everything and the conclusion of every matter. Everything You need in this life had been extensively said in this book. Unless you meditate on it, you will remain ignorant of all the treasures.

Beloved, meditate on it day and night and it will show you

how to fight all your battles. Everybody on this earth no matter the discipline, will find exhaustive instructions on the pages of this Book, if opened with an open heart.

Meditate on it day and night. Keep vigils at it till it unfolds to you. The things you meditate on will always manifest in your life. As you meditate on the words for a long time you tend to memorize them; and only then will you be able to declare and decree them in time of battles. If you keep on meditating what the BIBLE said: you are an overcomer, after sometime, you will begin to see yourself overcoming many bad things that have been pressing you down. Things like fear, failure, bitterness, anger and forgiveness.

According to Samuel Osaghae in Believers Daily Meditation, " Meditation creates a data bank for possible accessibility in times of need. When you are meditating on God's Word, you are creating a data bank, filled with relevant knowledge and information that the Spirit of God to make you an enviable model of a beneficiary of the dividends of salvation. The size of your data bank is dependent on your meditation. The more of God's Word you ponder on, the more expansion your data bank will experience as a result of the information you keep loading and meditating upon."

When you do not spend time on meditation, you will have a very small data bank with very little useful information. As such, anytime the Holy Spirit zooms into your data bank, there is nothing to download. But the man who meditated on God's Word daily will never be defeated by the challenges of life; he will always have an appropriate response to every card the enemy presents to him.

MEDITATION takes away your limit, and since the purpose

is to manifest, make sure you meditate on God's Word every day. So that you will experience profit and progress in your life.

CHAPTER 11
COMMAND THE MORNING

Beloved, learn to wake up early in the morning to study the WORD and worship God and hear His voice. After hearing His voice begin to command the morning.

Follow me to Job 38:12-13

"Hast thou commanded the morning since they days; and caused the dayspring to know his place;

That it might take hold of the ends of the earth, that the wicked might be shaken out of it.

Here, God is talking to you and asking you a question.

"Have you ever commanded the morning to release all it has for you?

For your information, this should be done early in the morning between 1 am and 5 am. Possibly, before the sun is out in the sky.

Verse 13 says when you do that the entire world comes under your control. Again, that the wicked shall be shaken out of the earth - that means that every wicked act, very incantation, every evil projection and every attack should be shaken out of your life.

See what Psalm 68:19 said.

"Blessed be the LORD, who daily loaded us with benefits,

even the God of our salvation.

So, everyday has blessings, but they are not coming to you, you have to command the day to release them to you.

Beloved, when God created mankind, He gave dominion to mankind over the sea, over the air and over the earth. Satanic agents know that God gave dominion to mankind, so they wake up early in the morning to command and conjure the day to answer them from negatively.

That is why every occult man and woman wakes up early in the morning to make incantation. The spiritualists, occult churches, witches, wizards, all wake up early in the morning to make incantation.

They command the wealth of the morning to answer them negatively. Remember, the devil comes to steal, kill and destroy.

When do they normally steal? Midnight! Every bad act is carried out at midnight.

Micah 2:1 Woe to them that devise iniquity, and work evil upon their beds! When the morning is light, they practice it, because it is in the power of their hand"

Have you seen what the BIBLE is saying? Because it is in their power they practice it. All you do is to decree and declare.

So get up early in the morning, study the WORD, praise and worship, and then go into intercession and lastly go into declarations and decrees.

Examples:

As I go out today no evil shall befall me.

I command this day every blessing due to me and my family to come to us.

Wherever I go today, everybody must give me audience.

Every evil programmed against me and my family I deprogram you

My dear, open your mouth wide and decree what you want. You can say to that mountain, be thou removed.

Psalm 18:45 said:

"The strangers shall fade away, and be afraid out of their close places."

Beloved, they shall hear your voice and fade away. When will they hear your voice? Early in the morning. So the morning has ears, if you start commanding the morning, you will take of every system, because it is your command you will receive

CHAPTER 12
CONCLUSION:

I encourage you my dear to spend more time with God. The more time you spend with Him, the more of the Holy Spirit you will have. You cannot be full of the Holy Spirit without prayer and without praying more than one hour you cannot reap say that you are full of the Holy Spirit. The devil is not afraid of your going to church, the devil would also be silent while you study the BIBLE. But the devil will resist you when you start praying.

When you pray the devil will cause trouble, but when you pray more, the devil will leave you. Yes, God knows about your problems. God has power to solve your problems but He is waiting until you pray about these problems.

Only through prayer can you overcome all the works of Satan and see the hearts of people become receptive when you saw the seed of gospel to establish the kingdom of heaven on them. Without giving yourself to much prayer, there can be no church growth!

Finally, it is important that you learn to plead the Blood over yourself, your family, siblings and loved ones before retiring to bed each night.

The Holy Spirit taught me to be going outside the house to plead the Blood of Jesus Christ, as I walk round.

As you pray in the night, always remember to offensively pray against the members of the Dark Kingdom before going to sleep. If you forget, you will be attacked in the spiritual realm during the night.

As you plead the blood, demons will depart, this is a weapon that no evil spirit, nor even Satan himself can stand against. Remember to use your legal right and spiritual authority. God had placed the enemies under your feet and given you power to tread on serpents and scorpions and over all the powers of the enemy; and nothing shall by any means hurt you.

Show no mercy to the enemy as you employ these strategies and tactics. God will cause you to triumph in Jesus Name Amen.

CHAPTER 13
REPENTANCE PAGE

THE LAST PAMPHLET

I heard a beautiful story that went thus:

-Every Sunday afternoon after the morning service in the Church, the Pastor and his eleven-year-old son will go through the town and hand out spiritual pamphlets.

One Sunday afternoon when it time for the Pastor and his son to go out to the street with the pamphlets, it looked very cold outside. It was raining at last and the boy dressed up in a warm cloth and said, "Ok, Dad I am ready."

And his daddy said, "Ready for what?"

"Dad, it is time to get the pamphlets and go out."

His father replied, "Son it is very cold outside, it is pouring down heavily."

The looked surprised and asked, "But dad will people not go to hell even not on rainy day?"

His father replied, "Son I am not going out in this cold."

Sadly, the boy asked, "Dad can I go please, let me."

His father hesitated before and later turned and said, "Ok, you can go."

"Take the pamphlets, take care Son."

"Thanks dad," then he went out to the rain.

This eleven-year-old boy moved from door to door of that city giving out pamphlets to everyone he saw.

After walking for two hours in the rain, he was soaked in wet, but had one last pamphlet left. He stopped at a corner and looked for someone to hand the pamphlet to but the streets were but the streets were totally deserted. Then he turned to walk to the first house he saw and walked from the side to the door and rang the bell. He rang the bell but no one answered, he rang again but no one opened the door.

He waited but there was no answer, finally the eleven-year-old soldier turned his back to leave. But something stopped him.

Again he turned the door rand the bell and knocked even louder on the door. He waited, something was keeping on that pouch. He rang again and this time the door opened slowly. Standing at the door was an elderly lady looking very sad.

She asked, kindly, "What can I do for you my son?"

With radiant eyes and a smile that light up the whole world, this little boy said,

"Ma, I am sorry am disturbing you, I just come to say that Jesus loves you very much and I come here to give you my very last pamphlet which will tell you all about Jesus and His great love."

Then he handed her his last pamphlet and turned his back to leave.

She called him and said, "Thank you son, may God bless you

so much."

The following Sunday morning Church, his father, the Pastor was behind the pulpit and as the service began he asked;

"Does anyone has a testimony or something to share."

Slowly at the back row of the Church and elderly woman came up and as she began to speak the glory of God transcended on her face.

"Nobody knows me in this Church, I have never been here before. You see before last Sunday I was not a Christian, my husband passed away some time ago leaving me completely in this world."

"Last Sunday being particularly a "rainy day", I have decided in my heart to end my life. I had no hope or one to love. So I took a rope and a chair and went on the stairs to the attic of my home. I tied the rope to the beam and stood on the chair, and fast the rope around my neck standing on my chair. When suddenly the sound of the front door bang startled me, I thought who in this world could that be. For a long time, nobody had ever rung my bell or come to see me, so I removed the rope from my neck and went to the door. When I opened and saw who it was I could not believe it, because on my front pouch was the most radiant and angelic little boy I have ever seen in my life.

His smile, oh I could never describe it to you. The words from his mouth caused my heart which was dead a long time ago to leap to life as he said with a treble-like voice. "Mum I just come to tell you that Jesus loves you." Then he handed to me this pamphlet which I am holding in my hands. As the little angel disappeared into the cold rain, I closed the door and read every word in the pamphlet. So I went up attic to get my rope and chair. I will not need them anymore. See I am now a very happy daughter of the King of Glory.

Since the address of your Church is at the back of the pamphlet I came here personally to say thank you, personally to the angel of God who at the right time delivered my soul from spending eternity in hell.

Everyone in the Church had tears in their eyes and a shout of praise and honour to the King echoed throughout the building."

The Pastor came down from the pulpit and headed to the front row, where his little angel was sitting. He took his son in his arms and sobbed uncontrollably- (source, unknown as at the time of this publication).

It is likely that no Church had ever had such a glorious moment and probable that such a glorious example of a father's love and honour. For His Son had ever been seen on this earth except for one other, this Father also allowed His Son to go to a cold dark world. He received His Son back with unspeakable joy. All heaven shouted praises and honour to the King.

This Father had placed His Beloved Son on a throne above all principalities and power and had given Him a name which is above every other name. Blessed are the ears that hear this message, do not let it be the last. Listen to it again, think about this. Put it into practice for God wants to use you and remember then how God can make the difference in the life of someone very close to you.

Having gone through the story, could you please close your

eyes and ask God to forgive you all your sins. Promise Him that you will never be involved in anything that will make Him regret ever creating you. Surrender your life totally to Him, depend on Him alone to save you. Only He can help you and protect you.

Let us pray: Awesome God, Father of all, Our Maker, Our Defender, Our Peace, Our Advocate, Omnipotent, Omnipresent, Omniscient God. Here are your children before your throne, You said in Your Word that anyone that comes to you, you will not wise cast away. Raise soldiers from these ones, who will take the Gospel to every corner of the world without fear. Those who will not compromise in time of percussion, those who will defend the Gospel not minding who is before them. We pray for unity among your children not minding the colour or the tribe. Let there be peace among your children as they work diligently in your vineyard. At last may they behold your face on the last day in Jesus name we pray. Amen.

PRAYER REQUEST

Water of Life and Fire Ministries

20/22 Osadebe Street

Ogui New Layout

Enugu Nigeria

08034617855

08025942028

ACKNOWLEDGEMENT

I will like to express my sincere gratitude to Ifeoma Edna Udem for her kind understanding and ability to put a smile on my face anyday, anytime.

My utmost appreciation goes to my God for providing the strength and wisdom required to complete this work successfully.

ABOUT THE AUTHOR

Ody Udem

Ody Udem is the Chief Executive Director of James Kay and Vicky International Foundation. Senior Pastor of Water Life & Fire Ministires, an author and a Marriage Counselor.
She has been on Widows Forum for years till 2010 when Water of Life & Fire Ministries was declared open.
With her experience in different forums like "Widows forum" and a marriage forum called "Peace at last Marriage Forum", she has provided successful counselling and direction to couples undergoing marital conflicts.
She is happily married with four children.

BOOKS BY THIS AUTHOR

Chimdi

Chimdi portrays the plight of the less privileged children of the world. They find themselves in horrible situations and only God-sent people will rescue them. Chimdi comes from a poor but honest family and she was brought up to be hard working and truthful. Just before the end of her primary school, her father died and the situation looked grim for her.

Domestic Conflict Resolution - Implementing The Win-Win Approach

Discover well-worn principes of conflict resolution in your marriage. In this book, kingdom strategies are provided which will give you a leverage in identifying hotspots in your marriage as well as learning to navigate these areas with ease where everyone becomes a winner; all can become victors and non-vanquished.

www.ingramcontent.com/pod-product-compliance
Lightning Source LLC
LaVergne TN
LVHW052054160826
845678LV00015B/3223

* 9 7 9 8 8 1 8 7 0 9 9 9 4 *